No good deed goes unpunished.

Amy knocked on the big tin door, listening to the echoes as they rattled away. "It's Doc Amy. Let me in."

No answer. She tried again. "Max? It's Amy? Are you there?"

Another silence. No, not silence. Some sort of creaking noise, then, off to the side, another door, one she hadn't noticed, groaned slowly open.

Amy dashed to it, only to find her way blocked by Audrey, who held out both arms. "Wait, child. They're bringing him out."

"Should they even be moving him?"

"They had to. Too dangerous for everyone."

But it was too late to ask why. A makeshift stretcher, a chunk of green canvas fastened between and looped around two lengths of two by four, was easing its way through the door. Dan was at one end, and Rob at the other. Max ducked through the door after them and pulled it closed behind him, looking extremely distressed. "I never thought Alan would do such a thing," he said. "I never thought, I didn't..." His words trailed off as he caught sight of her. "Do something, Dr. Duvall. Please." It was the first time she'd seen Max genuinely anguished.

But she was already there, staring at the blood, and the damage. "What *happened?*"

BOOKS BY M.M. JUSTUS

TALES OF THE UNEARTHLY NORTHWEST

Sojourn
"New Year's Eve in Conconully"
Reunion

TIME IN YELLOWSTONE

Repeating History
True Gold
"Homesick"
Finding Home

Much Ado in Montana

Cross-Country: Adventures Alone Across America and Back

New Year's Eve in Conconully

A Short Tale of the Unearthly Northwest

M.M. Justus

Carbon
River
Press

New Year's Eve in Conconully

New Year's Eve in Conconully

CHAPTER 1

Amy Melissa Duvall, known to all as Doc Amy, even though she'd been an EMT in her former life, not an MD, glanced around her office with satisfaction. Not that she saw many patients in this room; the good people of Conconully were used to having their doctor come to their homes instead of going to the doctor's office or the hospital. Given that there was no hospital within reach, temporal or practical, of the town she called home, it was probably just as well. And as an emergency medical technician, she'd been used to going to her patients rather than having them come to her, anyway.

But it was still good to have an office. It was the only part of her life she managed to be orderly in. Heaven only knew her personal life wasn't. Audrey had long since given up trying to teach Amy cooking on a wood stove and proper nineteenth century housewifery, and after only the one incident Belinda guarded her precious treadle sewing machine from Amy's touch as if the machine would poison her.

Well, perhaps not poison her. But Amy wouldn't put it past the monstrosity to run a needle through her finger. And then who would treat the doctor?

Her skills were every bit as valuable as Audrey's or Belinda's, though. Or those of young Louisa who, as part of the town's odd barter system, came to clean and tidy Amy's house every week. After all, until she'd arrived, Conconully hadn't had a medical person in – years. For a long time, anyway, even if she'd never figured out quite how to measure time in a place where time didn't exist.

Until she'd arrived. Amy still couldn't quite bring herself to think of what had happened to her as being brought here, even though, to the best of her knowledge, it was a more accurate way of stating the sequence of events. She still didn't know all the details, but seeing it happen to someone else had shown her how it *was* done, even if how it *could* be done was still less than clear.

Still, she was here, and she was happy as she knew she hadn't been in the wide world, and now, with Dan's arrival, she wasn't the only one from Outside anymore. She couldn't have said why that mattered so, but it did.

It didn't hurt that Dan was handsome and had the best smile on the planet, either. That he had a great sense of humor, which was absolutely essential for anyone living in this crazy place, the skills to fall right into the vital role of sheriff, and the easygoing nature to accept what had happened to him.

Well, now he had that nature. Perhaps because he'd seen what it was like to go back to the wide world and find out he no longer fit there.

Amy herself hadn't tried that one, and had no desire whatsoever to do so.

No. She belonged here, as she'd belonged nowhere else in her life or her world. She was meant to be here, no matter how she'd arrived.

And it was New Year's Eve, and she had a party to look forward to. Locking her office door behind her, she turned and jumped back in surprise at the man standing on her porch.

"Are you ever going to quit doing that?" she asked.

Dan grinned. "Don't see why I should. Come on, I'll walk you home."

"Around the corner? I don't know if I can make it that far by myself." But she took his arm, knowing he wasn't here for her safety. Barring a few mostly predictable exceptions, Amy was willing to bet Conconully was the safest place on Earth. He was here, she thought, flattered as she was every time he did something like this, because he wanted to be with her.

It was the one thing she'd regretted when she'd first arrived, and for some time after. She'd thought she'd be forever alone, forever on her own among friends. Then they'd brought Dan to her, and then she'd gone straight from regret to guilt, that they'd jumped in and ruined his life just for her.

But when he came back, on his own, and told her that his life Outside hadn't been worth living without her –

Well. She smiled up, and up, at six-foot-two-to-her-own-barely-five-feet Dan, who told her, "You can do anything you set your mind to. I've seen you do it." They strolled along in harmony, but when she would have turned in at her own front door, he added, "Max wants to see us," and kept going, his hand holding hers tucked firmly into his other elbow.

Amy felt her stomach clench. Her hand must have, too, because his expression changed from humor to determination. "What have you done now?" she asked lightly.

"Nothing. And if he–" Dan's mouth shut with an audible snap.

"If he what, Dan?"

His gaze down at her softened. With an effort, Amy guessed. "He's Max. He can do anything. Almost anything," he conceded. "But not everything."

"You're making no sense." But as they came around the corner onto Okanogan Avenue, little Philip Arngrim came tearing towards them from the opposite direction.

"Whoa, Phil!" Dan said, catching the child up in his arms. "Where're you going in such a hurry?"

The little boy, who was about six and had been ever since Amy'd first met him, was obviously distraught. Amy pulled a handkerchief out of her trouser pocket and reached for his tear-streaked face. "What's the matter?"

"Grandpa. He had an accident. He's hurt bad."

Dan only nodded, although Amy caught her breath. This wasn't – well, it hadn't happened before, at least not in her memory. "Where is he, Phil?"

"In the garage."

Amy looked up at Dan, but his gaze was on the little boy. "I'll go get my bag."

But Dan was already striding off, his long legs eating up the ground, Philip in the crook of his arm as if he weighed nothing.

The bag was in its normal spot, on the table just inside her office door. Having an orderly office paid off, even if she had to fight her own untidy nature to keep it that way. She grabbed it, not bothering to relock the door after her, and ran.

She'd gotten to the point over time where she could predict the normal illnesses and accidents that befell the citizens of Conconully, almost as if they were marked on a calendar. She'd even been able to cure some of them with the rudimentary medicines and equipment available to her. Since Dan had arrived, though, things had been changing. She'd been told the changes had actually started with her. She had no idea which ones, or in what way.

But this was different.

The garage was an odd place inside an odd place. Amy wasn't quite sure how Max managed to cause the affairs that happened in that garage to come to pass. She only knew what did happen there was important, that even Harry the pig's magic worked more strongly there than it did anywhere else.

And, so far as she knew, old Mr. Arngrim had no business there. Max was very picky about who he allowed into the garage and who he didn't. Rob, Audrey, and now Dan, and that was it. Even she hadn't been permitted to enter it, and she wondered if Max would let her inside to treat her patient. Surely he would.

Amy was out of breath by the time she reached the garage. It was at the other end of town, along the road that led through the canyon that was their only connection to the wide world. If one could even call it a connection, given that walking far enough down that road could kill a person. Or so she'd been told.

It hadn't killed Audrey when she'd gone to fetch Dan...

She knocked on the big tin door, listening to the echoes as they rattled away. "It's Doc Amy. Let me in."

No answer. She tried again. "Max? It's Amy? Are you there?"

Another silence. No, not silence. Some sort of creaking noise, then, off to the side, another door, one she hadn't noticed, groaned slowly open.

Amy dashed to it, only to find her way blocked by Audrey, who held out both arms. "Wait, child. They're bringing him out."

"Should they even be moving him?"

"They had to. Too dangerous for everyone."

But it was too late to ask why. A makeshift stretcher, a chunk of olive green canvas fastened between and looped around two lengths of two by four, was easing its way through the door. Dan was at one end, and Rob at the other. Max ducked through the door after them and pulled it closed behind him, extremely distressed. "I never thought he would do such a thing," he said. "I never thought, I didn't..." His words trailed off as he caught sight of her. "Do something, Dr. Duvall. Please." It was the first time she'd seen him genuinely anguished.

But she was already there, staring at the blood, and the damage. "What *happened?*"

She'd seen worse accidents, Amy thought, back in the real world. Car wrecks and mill accidents and that sort of thing. But not without access to real care, not without expectation of a helicopter on its way to carry the victim off to Harborview Hospital and its level one trauma center in Seattle. All she had here was herself, what she'd been able to reinvent and build, distill and brew. What she'd been able to cobble together on her own.

This was beyond anything she could do, and she knew it.

But people don't *die* here, she thought desperately. Not like this. Not even before Dan had stepped in and dealt with the rabid wolf once and for all had anyone *died*, exactly, even though they'd been just as gone as if they had. In all the time she'd been in Conconully, the closest anyone had come to real death was when Daniel first arrived in his totaled cruiser, his head injury serious enough that Amy had worried he'd never wake up.

Still. "Set him down. You shouldn't have moved him."

"We didn't have a choice, honey."

She didn't have a split second to spare for that inane remark. Dan had been a state trooper out in the real world. He'd seen accidents. He knew better.

Her patient was breathing, fast, shocky and shallow, but breathing. She had to stop the blood, somehow. She reached for her bag, for the pressure bandages some of the ladies sewed for her, to find one shoved into her hand. Peeling the blood-soaked edges of Mr. Arngrim's shirt out of the way, she placed the bandage and pressed it firmly to the wound, holding the ragged edges of his skin together.

"Here, let me do that." Dan's big hand came down gently next to hers.

"Thanks."

Mr. Arngrim moaned. Well, at least he *could* moan. Amy started at the top and worked her way down, searching for more injuries. Found nothing, but then anything else would have been redundant.

"All right. We need to get him to my office. I'll take the pressure – my God."

The bandage was soaked already, and more was oozing out from under it. She added another bandage on top of the first, and Dan moved his hand to accommodate it. "What did you *do?*"

Dan just looked at her helplessly. She didn't have a split second to convey the fear she was feeling, but she knew he understood. It was one of the reasons she loved him, most of the time.

"We have to get him to my office. I can't do anything about this here." She couldn't do anything at all, but she didn't want this lovely old man to die in the dirt.

"Grandpa!"

"Get that child out of here!" The boy's cries dropped out of her consciousness as she added her hands to Dan's to slow the bleeding. A third pressure bandage. A third. Such a small wound to bleed so much. "All right. Let go, Dan. I'll do this. You take the stretcher." Then, as Dan and Rob lifted Mr. Arngrim up again, "Not so high, fellows." She didn't add, I need to be able to reach. It was understood.

CHAPTER 2

Mr. Arngrim was still breathing by the time they made it back to her office and set him down on the bed. It was about all she could say for him, but Amy counted it as a major victory. He'd passed out about halfway back. She didn't know whether to be relieved that he wasn't awake and feeling what had to be agony, or even more worried than she already was that he hadn't roused.

"Dan, stay with me, please," she said as she went to her cupboard for the tools and supplies to examine the wound more thoroughly. Perhaps it was something she could simply stitch up. And perhaps the moon was made of green cheese.

But when– if he died on her, she did not want to be alone with him.

He couldn't die. This was Conconully, and he couldn't die. He could fade away, as others had done, but he couldn't *die*.

"What can I do, Amy?" Dan was on the other side of the bed, with a fresh bandage.

"I've got to look at the injury. See if there's anything I can do." She glanced up as a head poked in. "Keep everyone out, please."

"Sure thing." He glared at the head, which belonged to Audrey, and she muttered something that sounded like, "I just wanted to help," but backed away, closing the door behind her.

It wasn't a big wound. Obviously a puncture. It didn't look like much of a wound at all on the outside, except for the blood. The area around it was swelling, which meant that while they'd stopped the bleeding on the surface, that was all they'd done.

Warily Amy spread the edges of the skin open, and the blood pulsed out again. Copiously. And there wasn't a damned thing she could do about it. She was no surgeon, and even if she was she had no operating room, no equipment, no supplies, no anesthesia.

"What was he impaled on?" she asked Dan abruptly. "And why was it removed?"

He started. "A piece of metal. We had to remove him from it, because it was too big for the other way around."

"You know as well as I do that there's nothing I can do for him now." For form's sake, Amy soaked a dressing in water – no point in using alcohol as an antibacterial at this stage, all it would do was cause the poor man more pain – and removed the blood from the taut skin around the wound. Took a fresh dressing and applied it. And gazed up at her fellow refugee from the real world helplessly.

"But you have to. It's how you change things."

"I guess there's a first time for everything."

"Someone should go get his family."

"You don't think they're not out there now?" Amy reached down to touch Mr. Arngrim's forehead, which was already hot.

"They should have a chance to say good-bye."

"Yes."

Amy did not look up from Mr. Arngrim's slack, wrinkled face as Dan quietly let himself out of the room.

He was back within seconds. "Audrey's fetching them."

"Is Max out there?"

"Yes." Max, among other things, functioned as pastor of Conconully's church. Amy wasn't sure how up he was to comforting the grieving, but he was all they had.

"You probably ought to bring him in here, too." She didn't look up as Dan left the room again, as she re-covered the wound, shaking her head over the taut swelling around the hole left by whatever it was had impaled poor Mr. Arngrim.

She wondered how he'd gotten into the garage, what he'd been trying to do, how he'd managed to do such *damage* to himself. Why it was so dangerous in there, and why Max had let this terrible accident happen.

She wiped his face, and pulled a sheet up to the old man's chin. Smoothed his hair, and listened to his breathing, which was becoming more and more shallow, and less and less frequent. Wished she could do something, anything, to save him. But trying to open him up and repair whatever organs had obviously been ruptured would be far worse, under these circumstances, than doing nothing at all.

"You wished to see me, Dr. Duvall?"

Amy looked up to see Max as she'd never seen him before. The anguish was still there, written across his face, but the primary emotion she saw now was guilt. Guilt?

"What really happened, Max?"

He hesitated.

"I need to know," she added gently. "His daughter will be here any minute."

"Yes. Yes, I know. I'm not sure what happened. I'm not." He was responding to her disbelief, Amy knew, which had to be written across her face. "I'm not omniscient, in spite of what some people say. It was an accident. I didn't know he was there when we turned the machine on. I should have. I should have." He was getting more and more agitated. "He shouldn't have been able to enter the garage, and if he did, I should have known immediately. I didn't know. I didn't *know*."

Amy came around to him and led him to the wooden straight-backed chair in the corner. Pushed him into it, although it took alarmingly little effort to do so.

"It's all right," she crooned at him. "It's all right."

He looked up at her, his face stricken. "What have I done?"

It was just as well that Dan opened the door and ushered Dorothy Arngrim into the little room right then. If he hadn't, Amy would have felt obliged to try to respond to Max, now hunched in the corner and acting anything but pastorly.

"Get him out of here," Amy whispered to Dan as Dorothy stepped over to look at her father.

"What happened?"

"Not now." Amy tried to compose herself as she went to speak with her patient's daughter, and mostly succeeded, drawing on her

15

long-disused EMT experience at staying calm in situations that would cause any normal human being to run screaming in the other direction.

Dorothy was staring down at her father. "What's happening?" she asked in a bewildered tone.

"I'm afraid there's nothing I can do, Dottie," Amy said as gently as she could.

"No, I understand that. He was already beginning to fade, or at least that's what he told me. He said he'd had a bellyful of being an old man, and it was past time. But I didn't think he could do this." She looked up at Amy for the first time, tears streaming down her cheeks. "I didn't think any of us could do this."

"Neither did I." Amy looked over to where Dan was, having managed to pry Max out of the chair, having no success whatsoever in getting him out of the room.

"Max," Dorothy said, "you must know." She stepped around the bed and went to him. "Tell me."

Max took a deep breath. So, Amy noted wryly, did Dan. And Dorothy. And, as she let her own out after, did she.

"I don't know, Dorothy. I suspect it was your father's own will that allowed it. You knew how he'd been feeling since your mother left us?" Amy had never met his wife. She wondered just how long he'd been grieving for her in this place time forgot.

"Yes."

"You knew his wishes?"

"Yes."

A creaky-sounding inhalation drew them all back to Mr. Arngrim's bedside. Surrounding him, family, friends, those who cared for him.

Amy knew that sound. There was a reason it was called the death rattle. From the look on the faces of the three standing witness with her, Amy knew they recognized it, too, in spite of, so far as she knew, having not heard it since before the flood.

"He's a good man, Dorothy," Dan offered. "One of the best."

She smiled weakly at him. "Thank you."

Max put a hand on hers. "I am so sorry, Dorothy. But he led a good life."

"Yes."

Mr. Arngrim exhaled, and did not inhale again.

Dorothy turned her fingers to grasp Max's, and bowed her head. Max gave a tiny jerk of his head toward the door. Amy took the hint, and so did Dan. They slipped outside to find almost the entire town standing there in silence. Waiting for news, apparently.

Amy took a deep breath, but Dan reached for her hand and squeezed it. Before she could speak, he said, in a tone she'd never heard from him before, "He's gone."

CHAPTER 3

Of course she had to provide more explanation than that, and Amy did her best, but it was so hard to watch the people she'd – failed? changed? – realize the momentousness of what had happened. She and Dan watched as the crowd slowly dispersed, then, more weary than she'd been in longer than she could remember, she turned to go back inside. "I have no idea what to do now."

Dan kept hold of her hand. "Give them a little longer, kiddo," he told her. He drew her to the steps and down to sit on them. She was glad to get off her feet, as she was feeling more wobbly than she wanted to admit to.

"But what does happen when the first person in what? forever? dies? So far as I know we have no undertaker, no funeral home, no cemetery. What happens next?"

"What happened when the children died of rabies?" Dan asked. "From the wolf? This isn't the first time someone's died here, at least according to what you told me."

Amy stared at him, completely nonplussed.

He all but rolled his eyes. "Don't tell me. They pulled a Harry Tracy."

"I, I–" She didn't know what to say. She hadn't questioned it at the time, hadn't wanted to question it. *Should* have questioned it. But she hadn't.

"Please don't tell me those poor kids went through rabies every year."

Amy found her voice at last. "No. Only the one time. That I know of, at any rate. I don't," she faltered again, "I don't know. And I don't know what to do."

"I don't know, either," Dan said. "And I don't mean the funeral or whatever. Funny thing is, I don't think Max does, either. You didn't see him when the accident happened."

"No, I didn't," Amy replied, nettled by the reminder that even in dire circumstances she hadn't been allowed inside the garage. "What goes on in there, anyway?"

Dan drew her closer and put his arm around her. "Not much, really. Car repairs. Plans for the future."

Amy jerked her head up to stare at him. "*Car* repairs? Is that some sort of euphemism? And why you and not me?"

"I let Rob find me tinkering with some stuff a while back and he told Max." He looked sheepish. "I figured one of us ought to keep an eye on what they were doing in there. If I could have figured out a way to get you in, too, I would have, but everybody knows you have no talent in that direction."

Amy scowled at him, but then completely ruined the effect by snuggling in closer. She hated to admit it, but she wasn't sure if she could have handled this without him. Dan tightened his arm around her. "We'll get through this somehow."

The door opened, and Dorothy came through, her head bowed. Dan stood, pulling Amy up with him out of the way to let her pass. Max leaned through the doorway, gesturing at them to come in. Amy took a deep breath and headed for the door, more than conscious of Dan following close behind her.

She wasn't sure what to expect inside. Dan's comment about Harry Tracy had hit a nerve, and the children with rabies – it bothered her more than she could say that she could not *remember*.

Would Mr. Arngrim still even be there? Would he have faded away in spite of his injury? But no. He was still there, motionless on the bed.

Max looked up at her helplessly. Once again, Amy pulled stoic calm from that place deep down inside that she could not remember from her days out in the wide world. "Max, has this ever happened before? A death that's not part of the, I guess you'd call it rhythm?"

"No." He sounded stricken. "I shouldn't have– I shouldn't have–"

She cut him off. "That's not what I mean. I'm talking practically here. Has anyone had to deal with a body here before?"

She'd startled his brain into working, finally. "Not since the flood. There's a cemetery, just outside town, from back then. I'm sure Peter Phelps could make a coffin. But–" he gestured helplessly "–the body."

"I can deal with that," Amy said, resigned.

The door opened, startling all three of them.

"No, you won't," Belinda said firmly from the doorway, several of her cronies behind her. "You take care of the living. We will take care of the dead."

"Thank you," Dan said, in a more fervent tone than Amy would have expected. She glanced up at his relieved face. Relieved?

"You must not miss the party, Doctor Amy," Belinda went on, stepping into the room, followed by three other women. One carried rags and towels, another a suit of clothing. "Dan, would you please fetch us a bucket of water?"

Dan blinked, and headed toward the kitchen. Amy followed him. "Am I really to let those women do that grisly work?" she asked.

Dan only shrugged, shoved the bucket under the pump, and began to work the handle.

"And the party? They're still going to hold a *party* after this?"

"Yes," said a determined-sounding Max from the door. "We are. It's what Alan Arngrim would have wanted."

"But he's gone now," Amy said helplessly.

"Yes. And we will hold the party in his memory."

Dan lifted the now-full bucket from the sink and gave Max a wary look. "This isn't going to be like the flood party, is it?"

"Not in the sense you mean, no."

"No Harry the pig, no playing statues?"

"No." Max shook his head.

Dan shrugged, looking relieved again, and hefted the bucket as he carried it back into the other room. "All right."

Amy stared in consternation at Max. "You can't be serious."

Max gave her a wry smile. "And when, my dear, have you ever known me to be serious?"

CHAPTER 4

He meant it, Amy realized as she stood looking out her office window at the early winter sunset. Poor Mr. Arngrim's body was out of her office, thank God, cleaned and dressed and into a coffin delivered so quickly Amy suspected Peter Phelps had built it long ago and had it ready for old times' sake. Or maybe it was one left over from before the flood.

The bed in her little office was remade with fresh everything from the frame up, and the room was as pristine when Louisa had finished with it for the second time that day as it had been for the first time this morning.

Eight men had carried the now-heavy coffin to the church and placed it in front of the pulpit. People had lined the streets to watch the small sad procession. They'd laid bouquets of wax flowers, since even Cassandra could not come up with fresh flowers on New Year's Eve, on and around the coffin.

And then they had turned away, their sad expressions changing to determined smiles, to finish the preparations for Conconully's annual New Year's Eve party. It was macabre, Amy thought.

But if she'd had a nickel for every person who'd come to her and thanked her sincerely for her care of Alan Arngrim, then turned around and told her how much they were looking forward to seeing her at the party, she'd have been able to – what? Spend money in a place where money was irrelevant? She supposed she should consider herself lucky the party was distracting them and they weren't trying to load her down with baked goods and other gifts.

She sighed, locked up the office, and, alone this time, headed around the corner for home.

"The Mercantile looks like it did last May," Dan said, appearing nervous. Amy couldn't blame him for the comparison, because he was right. She couldn't even blame him for his uneasiness. This was his first big occasion since he'd come back to Conconully to stay, which had been something of a shock to him at the time.

But she did think he was overdoing it a bit. "Come on," she told him. "This is just a party."

He hung back. "It's weird, though, you know?"

"What's weird is that Max insisted the show must go on," Amy said. "And that everybody went right along with it."

Dan snorted. "Nobody ever says no to Max."

"I think Mr. Arngrim did." Amy shivered, even under all of her warmest finery. The long blue velvet dress, the knitted hood and mittens, the warm stockings and boots, and over it all, her battered shearling coat, the only possession she still owned from before. She knew it looked odd, especially when she wore the dress-up clothes Belinda insisted upon for special occasions, but it was hers. Sort of a lucky talisman, as she'd told Max, who'd read Belinda the riot act, or whatever. At any rate, while the seamstress still reserved her most disapproving glares for the coat, she no longer pestered Amy about replacing it with something more appropriate.

But Dan was asking her something. And tugging on her hand to get her attention. "I'm sorry. What did you say?"

"Do you really want to go in right away? It's a pretty evening. Let's go for a stroll first."

Amy stared up at him. "Now?" But the expression on Dan's face was almost pleading. This wasn't a request for an idle amble. Not here and not now.

"I-I can't help feeling like something weird's going to happen again," he said. She was right, Amy thought. This was more than mere nervousness.

"It won't."

Dan sighed. "I guess I'll have to take your word for it."

Amy wanted to sigh back at him. It had already been a long, hard day, and she'd long since forgotten how awful it was to lose a patient.

Not in the usual way of this place, but truly forgotten. Suddenly she realized Dan was offering exactly what she wanted.

"Sure," she said abruptly. "They won't miss us, and if they do I don't care."

"Great." He smiled down at her, but it didn't go all the way to his eyes.

"Come on then." She led the way down the street, away from the mercantile building, then glanced back. Among the small crowd at the entrance, Max stood in his top hat and tails, looking, as she always thought on such occasions, like a dapper little penguin.

Dan glanced back, too, and Max nodded. At him? At her? Well, she didn't need permission. Not from Max, not from anyone. One of the things Max was still getting used to, even now, was the fact that the newcomers he'd brought here were not as inclined to mindlessly obey him as – well, and at least one of the original citizens of Conconully wasn't either, not anymore. If any of them ever had been. Amy had her doubts.

Arm in arm, they headed away from the warmth and noise of the mercantile building, down the ever-less-tracked snowy street, until they reached Amy's little house once more.

"Do you want to come in?" she asked Dan. "I might be able to rustle up some hot chocolate."

"Maybe on the way back," he told her, taking a tighter hold on her when she would have headed for the door.

"The way back from where?" Now she was getting a bit concerned.

"Not far."

It wasn't as if they could go far, anyway. Or wanted to. "I've got my boots on, and I see you do, too. Planning this, were you?"

He didn't answer. The road – track, really – was pristine beyond her house, the snow free of human footprints. Not of critter tracks, though. Birds had crosshatched the surface in places, and paw marks, looking almost like the handprints of a small child, led to and from the congealing creek, betraying the existence of at least one raccoon.

When she would have stopped at the edge of the woods, Dan tugged on her hand again. "I want to go just a bit further," he told her. "Are you okay with that?"

Since Amy had a sneaking suspicion as to where he was headed, she nodded. "Don't worry," she answered what she thought was his unspoken question. "It won't have changed."

He gave her a curious glance, but didn't answer. Maybe he wasn't worried about that. The what the heck was he nervous about? He didn't think they were going to –

But as they climbed up and over the slight rise away from the creek, she could see the historical marker, not quite glowing against the luminous snow.

Dan headed straight toward it. Amy didn't know why she felt reluctance to go with him, but she ignored it. Not that she had much choice. His grip was firm enough to tow someone closer to his own weight than hers.

"Slow down." The snow was sticking to her skirts. She shook them with her free hand.

He glanced down at her. "Oh. Sorry."

"What's the big rush?"

"I don't know." He stopped in front of the marker, and so, of course, did she. He took a deep breath. "This just seemed like the right place."

"For what?" she asked. Now he did have her worried.

He grinned. "I've got you off-kilter now. Turnabout's fair play, I guess."

"Daniel Reilly, if you don't tell me what's going on right now, I swear I'll tie you up and leave you out here to freeze to death."

His grin broadened. "Sounds interesting. At least the first part does." He paused, the smile still playing around his lips, but his eyes gone serious. He let go of her arm, and Amy rubbed it.

"I'm sorry. I didn't hurt you, did I?"

All she could do was shake her head. "It's just cold." Without his warmth, she wanted to add, but stopped herself. He couldn't know how much she needed his warmth. He'd been here for – months, she supposed. It almost seemed as if they'd known each other forever now, but she could still remember the night he'd arrived, almost feet first.

They were good friends, she knew he liked her, and heaven knew she'd fallen for him from almost the first moment she'd met him, almost in spite of herself.

But she could never forget he'd been brought here. That they'd never have met if it weren't for Max, and Audrey, and the rest of the conspirators. He had come back on his own, but she still couldn't quite get past the fact that he'd been all but picked for her.

He reached into his pocket. Shoved the dry, light, powdery snow away from a patch of ground with one foot. And dropped to one knee before her.

Amy's mouth dropped open. By the time she could get her voice working again, he'd pulled his hand back out of his pocket, taken her mittened hand in his, and tugged the covering off. The crystal cold air bit at her skin for a second before he wrapped her hand in his.

"Amy?"

"Get up. Please get up."

Dan frowned. "I wanted to do this right."

"Why?"

He shrugged, apparently confused. "Because I want you to look back on this in a good way?"

"You don't–"

He stood suddenly. Amy let out her breath, feeling confusion, not relief, certainly not disappointment. But he wrapped her in his arms before she could sort her feelings out, and his warmth simply added to her befuddlement.

"You *are* cold. Coming out here was a dumb idea. I'm sorry." H pulled back and gazed down at her. "But that's the only stupid part. I hope." His gaze intensified, as if searching for something. "You know I love you, right?"

Amy gulped. She'd hoped, she'd wished, but she hadn't known for sure.

"I really am screwing this up, aren't I?" He wrapped her in his arms again. She pressed her cheek into the comforting scratchiness of his wool coat and breathed in his scent.

"All right, since you don't seem to know it," he said, let go of her and dropped to his knee again. "Amy Duvall, I do love you. It took me a while to quit being stupid about it, but when I went back to the real world? You were the one part of this place I regretted losing the most. More than anything. And you're the main reason I came back. I got back to Seattle and realized nothing there meant anything, because I wasn't here. With you."

Heaven knew what he was seeing in her eyes, but he sighed. "What can I do to prove it to you?"

"Max–" Amy said helplessly.

Dan growled. There was no other way to describe the sound. "Excuse my French, but screw Max. I want to marry you. I want to spend the rest of my life with you in this crazy place. I want us to be a family." He held out his fist and opened it, palm up. A ring glittered there. "Wear this for me, Amy. Please?"

"Where did you– no, I don't want to know." The ring was old-fashioned – of course it was, Amy thought. Old-fashioned and beautiful, sparkling in the starlight. She looked from it to him, to it, to him.

"Amy?" She'd put that new doubt in his voice. It was the last thing she wanted to hear in it.

She picked up the ring. "I think you're supposed to put it on my finger."

He shook his head. "Not till you answer me."

Amy didn't think she'd ever felt quite this way in her entire life. Certainly not in the real world, not even when she'd discovered she belonged here in Conconully. Maybe when she'd first seen Dan, before she'd stupidly thought he'd had his choices taken away. But she was having a hard time with all of this straight-out, positively naked emotion pouring off of him. Pouring out of her. "What part of yes don't you understand?" she asked him, projecting all the impudence she could muster.

He grinned. Plucked the ring from her fingers, and grabbed her hand. "I understand it all. Honestly." He slid the ring onto her finger. "See?"

She flung her arms around him. He bent and kissed her for a very long time.

CHAPTER 5

"This ought to be interesting," Amy said, on their way back to town. The air bit like ice, the stars sparkled overhead as if reflecting from the snow, and she couldn't remember ever feeling warmer.

"In what way?" Dan asked.

"It's another change. A big one. I wonder how people will take it." Honestly, much as she did love her, her fiancé – she couldn't help smiling at the term, not that she hadn't been already – he could be as dense as a box of rocks sometimes. But then he hadn't been here nearly as long as she had. He wasn't as afraid of rocking the boat as she'd become. "I wonder if we should even tell anyone yet, given Mr. Arngrim and all."

Dan turned and took both her hands in his. He'd put her mitten back on for her, but his finger rubbed the ring gently through the wool. "Seems to me like all the more reason to tell them. Something good to take away the bad." He paused. "Although they don't seem to need it. Come on. It's cold. We don't even have to go back to the party if you don't want to."

"But you want to."

They'd reached the edge of town, and the faint strains of music drifted out from the Mercantile.

"Yes, I do." He looked sheepish. "Part of me wants to crow like a rooster, as Audrey would say."

"Do hens crow?" Amy asked impishly.

That startled a laugh out of him, and she realized she was overthinking this. They strolled on, passing her house. It almost felt as if the music was drawing them. She let it.

And when they arrived back at the Mercantile, she wasn't the least bit surprised to find Max at the doorway. Still. Again? Was he worried? But she could see his eye caught by her hand in Daniel's, and his face lit.

"Yes, Max," Dan said.

Max grinned. "Glad to hear it. Come in, come in. We've missed you."

"You are *not* going to tell me you asked Max's *permission* to propose," Amy whispered fiercely.

"I wouldn't dream of it." But she didn't believe him.

"Wouldn't dream of what?"

But they were inside now, and engulfed by the music, the voices, and the sound of dancing on the polished wooden floor.

They shed coats and hats and scarves and, more reluctantly than she would have liked, mittens, in the vestibule. Amy took a deep breath as they stepped into the enormous room.

Betsy Fogle stepped forward. "Congratulations!"

"Er, what?" Amy'd put her left hand on Dan's arm as a matter of course. Now she tried to pull it back, but he hung on. "Too late now," he mouthed at her, then pitched his voice to be heard through the sound of good times. "Thanks! She said yes!"

Amy could have sworn the little three-piece band who played for all of Conconully's parties chose that exact moment to stop. And that every face in the building turned toward them.

Too late now was right. And she couldn't quite remember why she'd been so reluctant to tell everyone. No one seemed to think it in bad taste to announce a beginning so soon after such an ending –

Oh, she thought suddenly, and gripped Dan's arm.

"Are you all right?"

"Yes." It was the way things worked here. She knew that, had watched the changes happening in the town, especially since Dan had arrived. Max had sat her down and told her about them, that they were a good thing, that it brought them closer to the real world they'd all missed so much.

But she hadn't thought about what those changes could really mean. That they couldn't pick and choose from them, select only the ones they wanted.

Would Dan even have been able to propose to her tonight if poor old Mr. Arngrim hadn't chosen to go into the garage this afternoon, with those awful results? Was that the price they paid?

And was it a price at all? He was gone to be with his wife, who had died of a fever days before the flood. He'd spent an eternity in, did he think of this place as purgatory? Apart from the woman he'd loved, by all accounts, with all his heart. He thought of this place as more like hell, she suspected.

"Amy?"

"I'm fine," she lied, feeling as if she'd been hit by a very large brick.

"Amy," said Max, "come over here and sit down. No, Dan. I'll bring her back to you in a bit."

Max took her by the elbow, and her other arm slipped from Dan's. Blindly she went with him.

She wasn't quite sure how he'd managed it – well, Max being Max, she didn't need to know – but somehow he found a quiet corner with a bench, and settled her down upon it. Amy reached out blindly, and realized her hand was resting on Harry the pig, who wasn't in his usual niche in the Mercantile's bay window.

She ran her hand over Harry's rough plaster-like surface, her ring catching slightly on the texture. It was ridiculous to find the statue comforting, but she did. She saw Max was pleased, glancing over at him where he sat on her other side.

"You are happy, aren't you?" he asked her.

"I shouldn't be." She swallowed and turned her gaze back to the pig. "We lost a good person today, and it feels selfish of me." She stroked Harry again. "I didn't want to tell everyone at least until after the funeral."

"What changed your mind?"

"Nothing. It just happened. Betsy noticed my ring and, well."

"You could have taken it off before you came in."

"And hurt Dan's feelings?"

"Which means you do love him."

She glanced up at him again and saw that he was smiling. "Yes. Very much. I meant to thank you for bringing him–"

His expression changed and he interrupted her. "No. I do not take responsibility for Daniel's arrival, nor do I want it. He would not have come here if he didn't belong."

"So you've told me."

"And Alan Arngrim would not have – done what he did, either, if you and Daniel had not created the changes that allowed him to finally go be with his wife. Do you not think he was grateful?"

She hadn't thought of it that way.

"We're turning back into a real place now, Amy. With life and death and change. That's *good*, don't you see?"

What she saw was a man who felt responsible for how Conconully had come to be what it was, and so guilty about that responsibility that it bowed him over. She'd come to love the little man, almost like the father she'd never really had, and – would she do anything to relieve his guilt? Even let people die?

You did not *let* Alan Arngrim die, she told herself firmly. He was beyond your skill to save, you knew it and Daniel knew it. No one blames you.

"Nobody else is going to die anytime soon, right?" Amy asked the question lightly, but her feelings on the subject were anything but light.

"I can't predict the future. Not any more." He sounded positively relieved.

"Oh." Amy risked a glance up at him. "Well, it's not a talent I'd have wished on my worst enemy."

"I would hope I'm not your enemy."

Impulsively she wrapped her arms around him and squeezed him till he squeaked. "Of course you aren't."

"Hey, should I be jealous?" Dan said.

Reluctantly she let go, and smiled up at her fiancé. Then stood up and went to him. Dan wrapped an arm around her, and she around him. He felt warm and solid. More than he had before today? Perhaps.

She looked down at Max. "Happy New Year."

He smiled back up at them, his eyes alight. "Go on," he told them. "This is a night for celebration, and I want to watch you dance."

AFTERWORD

Thank you for reading "New Year's Eve in Conconully." I hope you enjoyed it. Reviews help other readers find books. I appreciate all reviews, whether positive or negative.

Would you like to know when my next book is available?
You can sign up for my new release email list at
    http://mmjustus.com/list,
or follow me on on Facebook at
    https://www.facebook.com/M.M.Justusauthor
on Twitter @mmjustus, or
on Pinterest at http://www.pinterest.com/justus1240/

"New Year's Eve in Conconully" is a short story in the Tales of the Unearthly Northwest, following the novel *Sojourn* and succeeded by the novel *Reunion*, both of which are available in electronic and print versions from many vendors including your local bookstore,

If you would like to read an excerpt from *Reunion*, please turn the page.

REUNION

LOST IN TIME

The year is 1910, and unemployed teacher Claudia Ogden is at the end of her rope. With nowhere to go and no one to rely on, she has no future at all. On the rumor of a job in a small, remote town called Conconully, she decides to bet what's left of her life on it.

But when she arrives, and is hired, to her relief, what at first seem like small eccentricities loom ever larger and more inexplicably, mysteries that make no sense. That is, until she meets Conconully's accidental magician, who wants her to save them.

But from what?

CHAPTER 1

"Please, Miss Ogden, sit down." The principal's voice was kindly but sad, as was her smile, If I hadn't already known the news was going to be bad simply because I had been called into her office, it was as certain now as the pain. And that pain was a fact of life. Had been since before I'd taken this new job in Seattle, almost a year ago now. But it had worsened to the point that I'd missed days of classes, unable to rise from my bed. Too many days. Which was why I was here, now, sitting in Miss Taylor's office, waiting to be told they'd have to let me go.

"Have you seen a doctor?"

"Yes." I had finally, at Jean's insistence, used the money I owed her for rent and made an appointment, for all the good it had done me. Now I was in debt to her and no better off for it. Worse off, given what was about to happen to me.

"Was he able to discern what the problem is?" Perhaps she was hoping I'd tell her he was curing me. Maybe she wanted to keep me. If nothing else, it would save her the trouble of hiring someone else.

But no. Dr. Spencer had been useless to me, for all he'd tried to hide the fact. I'd seen it in his eyes. I swallowed. "I-it's female troubles, ma'am."

Her face grew grim. "You're not with child, are you?"

My breath left me in a whoosh of a "No!" But her expression did not change, and I could feel the hopelessness settling into my soul along with the pain that even now was making it difficult to keep my back straight and not bend me over. I shook my head, to add to the emphasis. If only that was the problem. But whatever trouble was in my womb, the doctor could not determine what it was, and could not do anything.

"Will you be well soon?"

I shrugged helplessly. "I don't know. The doctor doesn't know, either."

Her brow furrowed. "Will you be going to a specialist?"

Dr. Spencer had broached the subject, but I could not afford it, not on a teacher's salary. "No, ma'am."

Miss Taylor's expression faded into something resembling pity. I supposed I did seem pitiful to her, but I could not muster the dignity to deny it.

"You have missed six days in the last month, and more than two weeks since term began two months ago." She paused, as if she didn't want to do what I, or my illness, had forced her to do. "I am sorry, Miss Ogden."

I blinked my stinging eyes, determined not to shame myself in front of her. Not any more than I already had. "Yes, I know. I will gather my things."

I had reached the door and put my hand on the knob when she said, "You are one of the best teachers I've ever had the pleasure to work with. I wish you well, Miss Ogden."

At least I made it out of the building before the tears began to fall.

"That witch!" Jean exclaimed. "Why not kick you to the gutter as well as knocking you down?"

"It was not her fault." I sank into one of the two armchairs flanking the fireplace. The parlor of the little house in west Seattle I shared with my friend and landlady was a warm and cozy space.

Three steps took Jean across the room. She turned back to face me. "They have an obligation to help you, Claudia, not to make things worse."

I stared at her. I should have expected something like this from Jean, whose thoughts on the subject of employee/employer relations put her somewhere on the far side of the radical Wobblies. The Industrial Workers of the World had caused a general strike in Seattle a few years ago, and, from what I understood, had not accomplished a thing besides bringing the city to a standstill. But I had not expected it. I had expected her to take my side, and be sympathetic, and do all the normal things one's friends do when one stumbles over misfortune. But no. She had to make even my illness someone else's responsibility.

"The district cannot afford to keep a teacher who is too ill to teach."

"Then they should pay for the care that will make you well again. Your principal said you are the best teacher she's ever worked with."

I should not have told Jean that, but it was the one bright spot in this awful day. "One of the best, yes." I could not help smiling.

She did not smile back at me. "And yet she let you go because you are too ill to work. Have you made an appointment with that specialist yet?"

I did not reply, but she apparently saw my answer in my face, because her frown deepened into a scowl. "If you do not, I shall do it for you."

"Jean—"

But she rode right over me. "What was his name? Dr. Whittington?"

"Jean—"

But she was already on the telephone, speaking with the operator. While I wished I had the strength, or the determination, to stop her, I sank back in the chair in defeat.

She went with me, too. "To make sure you don't back out," she told me. Jean was a good friend. Bossy and overbearing and thoroughly convinced she always knew best, but a good friend. And when the appointment was over, and payment was mentioned, she glared me down and produced the cash herself.

It wasn't charity, I told myself. But it was. And I was so beaten down by what the specialist had told me I let her do it. She knew my situation from that alone, even though I'd been fighting to keep my despair from my face the moment I walked out of the examining room. The doctor had performed enough humiliating and, as it turned out, unnecessary scrutiny to tell me what my heart had already known before I left Montana last year. After all, wasn't that the main reason I'd left in the first place? Perhaps not the main reason, as I had wanted the adventure, and to relieve my parents of one more burden as well. After all, my intellect, such as it was, had refused to believe what my heart knew until I could ignore it no longer.

Jean did not say anything until we reached our house – her house, really, as I was simply her tenant as well as her friend, and would not be either, or anything, much longer – and the door closed behind us.

She waited, until I fell more than sat into that same wing chair where she'd bullied me into going to the appointment where I'd heard my sentence. Then she said, more gently than I'd ever heard her before, "That bad, is it?"

I nodded, tried to speak, couldn't, and she sank down on the arm of the chair, putting a warm arm around me. "I am so sorry, my dear." She leaned away from me, as if ashamed of her kindness, and added in a tone more like herself, "What will you do now?"

Because of course I could not batten on her charity forever. "I don't know. Go home, I guess."

"You are home," she told me firmly.

It was kind of her, but no. "I meant Montana." Not that I could batten on my family, either. They could not afford to take me in, not with six other mouths to feed and my father's work tenuous at best.

"Is that what you want?"

Of course it wasn't, and she knew it. What I wanted was my job, my home here, my friends, Jean. My normal life. But it had been snatched from me by my incurable female troubles, by this – cancer, the specialist had called it – growing in my womb. He had offered surgery, to remove it, but said it had probably already grown to other parts of my body. If I had come in when I'd first felt the pain, I might have had a chance, but now... He'd trailed off, his expression almost accusatory, as if it were my own fault I'd gotten sick, that I hadn't had the money to come see him, let alone the time and money to let him cut into me–

"No, but I cannot stay here."

"No, you can't."

Well, that was clear and sharp enough. And cold. I jerked myself up out of the chair. "I will gather my things." I had no idea where I would find the money for the train ticket, but at least my parents would be more sympathetic than this. I had thought she was my friend, no, she had been my friend. I hadn't known she was going to turn so suddenly cruel.

"No!" Jean's hand came down on my arm. "That's not what I meant and you know it."

I could not help but stare at her. Her voice was choked, and her eyes brimming. "I do not wish you to leave. I wish more than anything that you could stay."

"I-I know." And oddly enough, I did believe her. Whatever her reason for wanting me gone, I knew it was not because she did not care.

Her brows came together. Her mouth set, and she straightened her shoulders. "I know where you can go. They'll help you there." As I continued to stare at her, speechless, she told me, in the tone I'd long since learned not to even try to gainsay, "And you will go. If I have to drag you there myself."

Well, and what else could I do? I could not fight both Jean and my pain. Nor the despair born from the hopeless diagnosis the doctor had given me. The three combined to put me to bed, where I lay curled like a homunculus, breathing through the throbbing ache in my womb, unable to think, or even wonder. I heard the front door thump closed as Jean left the house.

I must have slept completely through the night in spite of everything, because the shadows were at an early morning angle through my bedroom window when I woke. Jean was standing in the doorway, a satisfied look on her face. "They'll take you," she said. "I knew they would."

"Who?" I started to ask, but she had opened the door to my wardrobe.

"Where is your valise?"

"Under the bed. Jean–"

But she was already there. "Your train leaves in two hours."

I had stared at her before, but this was sheer disbelief. "My train where?"

She dragged my valise out, opened it, and started packing my things with the practice of long experience. As an aspiring Nellie Bly – not that she called herself that but it was what she was – she was used to packing her bags on a moment's notice. It was, she'd told me when she'd first invited me to live here, why she wanted a housemate: to watch over her things and have someone living in the house while she was gone.

She glanced up at me, grinning. "Conconully."

"Conco–" I stumbled over the unfamiliar name.

"Conconully. It's a tiny place, out in the middle of nowhere, but you grew up in Montana, so that shouldn't be a problem for you. They need a schoolteacher, and have for a long time–" she hesitated briefly "–and it should suit you right down to the ground."

Startled out of my, well, startlement, I asked, "How would you know that?"

"You always told me the one thing you missed about Montana was teaching in a one-room schoolhouse instead of being nothing but a cog in a machine." She frowned. "A machine that threw you out as soon as you needed repair." The frown disappeared as she concentrated on folding another dress into my valise. "Conconully's an odd little place, but the people are friendly. It's where I grew up–" another little hesitation "–and I'd have stayed if I could, but there's no work for a journalist there." Her expression turned peculiar, then she turned back to my now-almost full valise, muttering, "except for one story, but nobody'd believe me."

"Jean, do they know about my, my–" now it was my turn to hesitate. I could not bring myself to say the words, do they know I am dying?

"Yes, they know you're ill. It's all right, Claudia." She looked up at me again, her eyes brimming. "Please, do this for me. It's all right."

And so it was that a little over two hours later, I found myself on a train headed east on the bridge over Lake Washington, away from my dearest friend, who had stuffed an assortment of tickets into my pocketbook and told the conductor to watch over me. She'd hugged me one last time and made me promise once again that I would use them all and follow her instructions to the letter.

I had promised I would. Heaven help me.

CHAPTER 2

I almost felt as if I was going home, once the train crossed the pass to the east side of the mountains. The forest changed from firs and maples so dense with undergrowth that I could not see far beyond my window, to the pines scattered across parklike golden meadows the autumn rains already soaking Seattle would never touch. Snow fell gently over the pass but had not yet reached here, although when I touched the window, the glass was cold.

The conductor had taken one look at my ticket and said, "Just to Wenatchee, miss?"

All I had been able to do was nod. I had not had the chance, or the time, to look at the small stack of pasteboard slips wrapped in a piece of paper torn from one of the lined newsprint pads Jean used for her writing. Once I was settled into my seat, I was almost afraid to look at them, for fear I would be tempted to follow her instructions.

But, except for the bit of cash that had not so mysteriously appeared in my pocketbook, the tickets were the only currency I had. Reluctantly, I unfolded the paper, and read.

"Dear Claudia,

I know you think I've lost my mind, and I half suspect you're already thinking about cashing the other tickets in and seeing how far the money can take you. Please don't. If the world in general, and your former employer in specific (who makes me want to be very unladylike and spit on her for telling

43

you in one breath that you're the best teacher they've ever had and in the next that you're not worth what it would take to help you) are determined to make your life miserable, then I wish to do for you what you really deserve.

What did she think I deserved? To live? I still did not understand what she thought sending me away to this place would accomplish. Even if they gave me a job, I would not be able to keep it. And then where would I be?

Can you trust me? Please? I know trust isn't something you're used to doing, but just this once?

It was not a matter of trust. I was dying, according to the specialist. Something evil was growing in my body, something uncurable. I did not wish to die alone in a strange place. But I could not go back to the little house in west Seattle. Jean had made that abundantly clear, and I had nowhere else I could go there. I could not go back to Montana. I had not even had the chance to tell my family about my misfortune, nor did I wish them to know. They could do nothing for me, and it would only upset them. I leaned back in my seat and stared out the window at the rolling sagebrush hills that had taken the place of the open pine meadows. The late autumn sun glinted low in the sky, almost hurting my eyes. What could I do?

I read on.

When you get to Wenatchee, take one of the hansoms to the steamboat dock. The second ticket will get you aboard the Columbia Belle, and a berth where you can rest. The boat will arrive in Brewster in the morning. At Brewster, you'll need to get to the stagecoach station on the main street – Brewster is tiny, it's only a five-minute walk from the dock. The third ticket is for the stage to Omak.

Now it gets a bit odd. The morning after you arrive in Omak – I recommend the Wiggins Hotel, not that you'll have much choice in the matter, and get as much rest as you can – you'll need to go to the riverfront again, and find a teamster named Oscar Miller. He'll take you the last of the way to Conconully.

When you get to Conconully, ask for Max Pepper. Tell him Jean sent you. Everything will be all right. Take care, dear. I know you don't understand now, but you will. And perhaps I'll see you again someday. It is my fondest wish.

Jean

Yes, I was weary. And overwhelmed. And every rattle of the train hurt. And I still did not understand why Jean had done all this for me. Or why she had spent so much money to do it. It was hard to be grateful, as I supposed she thought I should be. But as she had said about the hotel in Omak, I did not have much choice in the matter. I would go to this town Conconully, and, if they would hire me after they saw how ill I really was, I would take the teaching job. I would earn a living at the one thing I loved more than anything for as long as providence allowed me to do it, and if nothing else, I could be of use to a town so isolated that they would take the likes of me as a teacher. Perhaps one of my students would go on to great things, and would remember my help. It was the only immortality I was likely to have.

The rest of my journey ran far more smoothly than I had expected. The hansom driver at the Wenatchee station took one look – and pity, I suspect – on me, and I arrived at the steamer dock with time to spare. The steward took equal care, and the cabin he led me to was far nicer than I had thought it would be. I sank onto the small but surprisingly comfortable bed in the tiny room it seemed I was to occupy all by myself. Utterly exhausted, I fell asleep before the sun sank below the mountains.

We arrived in Brewster the middle of the next morning, and again, people were far more helpful than I had any right to expect. I was on the stage out of town after a noon meal at a tiny shack the steward had recommended, that had tempted even my dulled appetite.

I wondered, as one gentleman assisted me onto the stage as a second put my valise in the boot, if I would regret the meal. The coach was dusty and rather battered-looking, and I suspected the road to Omak would be rough.

As all stagecoaches are. But I was still so weary, in spite of the sleep I'd had, that I do not remember much of the ride. I woke with a jerk when the stage stopped.

"Have a good nap?" The gentleman who had helped me to my seat smiled down from where he sat next to me, and I realized I had been resting my head on his shoulder.

"Oh!" I said, "I am sorry."

"Nothing to apologize for. You look a bit puny. Are you all right?"

I was not about to answer that question truthfully. "Yes, thank you. Where are we?"

"Omak."

"Already?" But I realized the light was fading outside and the air was nippy. Exactly how long had I slept? At any rate, I was glad for having done so. I was holding up better than I would have expected, in spite of everything.

"This where you get off?"

"Yes. Thank you." This as he rose to assist me down from the stage, and went to retrieve my valise.

"Thank you," I said again and reached to take it from him.

"Where're you headed?"

I shook my head to clear it. It did not help much. "I need to find somewhere to stay for the night."

"Goin' on from here in the morning?" I don't know what he saw in my face at his question, but his smile turned wry. "Sorry, miss. Woman travelin' alone might want a protector, but you don't know me from Adam, do you?" He shifted my valise to his other hand – where was his luggage? – and held his right hand out to me. "I'm Walt McMillan. Let me help you to your hotel, at least."

I took his hand. It was warm and firm and calloused. "Thank you." And then I remembered. "My friend recommended the Wiggins Hotel."

"Your friend's got good taste."

And so yet another kind stranger helped me find what turned out to be a pleasant establishment overlooking the river. I spent rather more of Jean's money for the room than I would have liked, but I felt safe there. In the event, I was in enough pain that evening so as to be of no use for finding another.

I suppose it was the ache that wearied me enough to put me to sleep. I woke early, feeling better, at least for the time being. After a breakfast I knew I needed but barely choked down, I bundled up against the cold and made my way carefully down the dusty main street running parallel to the river to the only dock I could see. It was perched on a bit of a point sticking out into the river, with two cargo steamers pulled up each to one side. A constant parade of men carried barrels on their backs or toted boxes and sacks. They traipsed up and down the dock and the dirt track leading up from it to a large warehouse, its wooden walls gray with weathering. A man in dirty worn overalls and a felt hat stood at its entrance, directing them.

I did not know who else to ask. The clerk at the hotel this morning had claimed no knowledge of anyone named Oscar Miller. Hesitantly, I approached the man.

I had to clear my throat twice before he noticed me, and then he only did so when one of the laborers jerked his head in my direction as he was taking his instructions.

"Yeh?" He sounded impatient, so I answered as quickly as I could.

"I'm looking for Mr. Oscar Miller, from Conconully. Do you know where I might find him?"

I had not been expecting the shocked stare he was aiming in my direction now. "What do you want with Miller?"

It really was none of his business. I repeated myself, wondering if something had happened to the poor man and if something had, then what would I do?

At last he shook his head. "Your funeral." He pointed to another building a bit further down the road.

Building was too kind a word. A pile of silvery gray worn planks leaned precariously as if in search of something sturdier to hold it up. I glanced back at the man, but he was already directing the next several laborers as to where to put their loads.

I shrugged, picked up my valise, and trudged toward it.

I hardly expected to see anyone working in such a place, but as I approached the ware– shack, I suppose I could call it, I saw a the rear end of a wagon sticking out from behind it, the back side of its box lowered to create a slope for loading. The wagon was almost full, mostly with barrels, but with boxes and crates and a few large sacks as well. I stepped forward to get a better view, and saw eight mules – healthy, glossy-looking beasts, hitched and ready to go. Obviously prepared to pull a heavy load. Even as I admired the animals, a man appeared from behind the shack, rolling another barrel in front of him.

He was old. Not just the kind of old-before-his-time from doing manual labor all his life like my father, but too old for the work he was doing. The barrel was obviously full, and had to have weighed more than he did, but he pushed and strained and used a slat as a lever, and manhandled that barrel up the ramp onto the wagon. He straightened, leaning against it to keep it from rolling back down and rendering all of his effort moot, and put a hand to the small of his back.

I could see he was breathing hard. I could also tell the moment he saw me. He turned away, and with an equal effort, tipped the barrel up on end and nudged it to join its fellows. But in the instant before he did, I thought I saw his eyes widen.

I stepped forward. "Mr. Miller? Are you Mr. Oscar Miller?"

Any fear I had harbored that he would not acknowledge my existence was relieved when he turned back to look down at me. "Who wants to know?"

It was not exactly the kindness I had been surrounded with until this morning, but I forged on. "My name is Claudia Ogden. I was told you might be able to take me to Conconully."

He stared rudely at me for a long moment. At last he said, "I don't know what you're talking about."

He had to. Or he had to know who would. "You are not Mr. Miller? Do you know where I can find him? My friend Jean Clancy said he would be able to help me."

His eyes widened briefly again, but he shook his head, as if trying to decide whether giving me his name would cause more harm than good. "I'm Miller." I had the very strong impression he wished he could have said otherwise.

Relief washed over me. "Oh. I am so glad. Can you take me to Conconully? Miss Clancy said you would."

He shook his head again. "No, I can't." He looked me up and down. I knew my distress was written across my face. My troubles chose that moment to give me a particularly sharp throb of pain, and it was all I could do to keep my back straight. "Go back where you came from, city girl. You don't know what you're getting into out here."

If only I could. "I have nowhere else to go. I will pay you–" No. My pocketbook was almost empty. Had Jean known this lack would push me on when nothing else could? "I do not have the money yet, but as soon as I start working again I will."

An odd expression flitted across his face, but it vanished before I could make sense of it. I could not decipher it except to understand somehow that he could take me, and he would not tell me why he would not.

"Please, sir. I-I have nowhere else to go."

Now I did recognize the expression on his face. Pain of his own. "I can't help you, young lady," he said at last. "And I don't know of anyone alive who can."

After a few more moments of utter silence, he went for another barrel. I watched him load that one, then another, and when he stopped to catch his breath again, I took a deep one of my own. "Where are you going with this load?"

He sighed and finished loading the barrel. "I can see you won't believe me without the proof of your own eyes."

"Should I?" I asked him. "Would you?"

"Prob'ly not." He turned back to look at me again, one foot propped on a wheel spoke. After a moment he seemed to come to some conclusion.

I tried not to look as desperate as I felt. "What have you to lose?"

That startled a rusty chuckle out of him. "You've got a point, young lady. All right. I'm almost done here. But it's your funeral."

It was the second time I had been told so this morning. Before today I had not heard anyone use that expression since my grandfather, who had died when I was a child. I sincerely hoped Mr. Miller did not mean it literally. I was close enough to that state as it was.

CHAPTER 3

After he loaded the last barrel, Mr. Miller took my valise, tucked it underneath the backless, cushionless, wagon seat between the two barrels helping to hold it up, and assisted me onto the hard wooden bench. I was grateful to be off my feet, but I sincerely hoped Conconully was not far, as this was not much of an improvement and my endurance was at a low ebb.

He strolled around to the other side by way of his mules, stopping to pat and give a good word to each of his obviously well-tended animals.

If it were not for those mules, and those creatures no rational reason at all, I think I would have scrambled back down, even with nowhere else to go. If it were not for those mules, that is, and for Jean's insistence. And now, I was beginning to realize, for my own curiosity.

It was as if Jean had set me off on some sort of quest, and everyone I had come into contact with since I'd left Seattle had been told to help me on my way. Everyone except Mr. Miller, that is, and even he hadn't discouraged me so much as given me a reason to fight to get my way. I could no more have gone anywhere else now without finding out what all the mystery was about, than I could have flown over the mountains.

I watched the old teamster surreptitiously watching me as he finished checking his sturdy mules and climbed onto the seat next to me.

I put my handbag down between my feet, Mr. Miller picked up the reins, and, with a jolt, the wagon began to move.

We soon left the little town of Omak behind, climbing up the steep bluffs west of town on a road that began as a graveled street, dwindling down to a dirt lane and then to nothing more than two worn wheel tracks running through the grass. The mules took the climb in stride, pulling the wagon with an easy effort, encouraged by Mr. Miller's occasional comment and light hand on the reins.

The late autumn wind whipped down off of the snow-capped peaks to the west with a dry cold completely unlike the damp chill of Seattle. The tall grasses brushing the sides of the wagon were stiff with hoarfrost, sounding like brooms sweeping across a wooden floor as we moved along. But the sky was a brilliant clear blue, the air was crisp, and, even as I tucked the ends of my scarf more securely around my neck, and pulled my hood forward to cover my ears, I breathed in deeply.

The air tasted almost like home.

Please do not mistake me. I liked Seattle. It was the biggest city I had ever seen, lively and important and full of mischief and inspiration. And beautiful, surrounded by water and mountains, with the grand peak of Mount Rainier towering above everything on the southeast horizon when the weather was clear, which was seldom enough most of the year. But it lacked horizons. Unless one strolled onto the beach at Alki, or rode a Mosquito Fleet boat out onto the Sound, heading for one of the islands or the isolated towns across the water, it was difficult to see any distance for the hills and thick forests.

Here, as I turned and looked behind me when at last we reached the top of the bluff, I could see almost to Montana, or so it seemed. Down to the river, where the twin towns of Omak and Okanogan clung to the shore a mile or so apart, across the river to the black cliffs and the rolling landscape beyond.

"Goes on forever, don't it?" said my companion at last when I turned around, sounding as if now that he had given in, there was no point in being surly. "Sure that's not the direction you want to be headin'?"

Ahead of us lay the eastern foothills of the Cascade Mountains, a wide valley between rolling hills. Not quite as wide a horizon, but still crisp and clear, unlike the moisture-blurry air west of the mountains.

Off in the distance, I saw animals, a good-sized herd. I pointed, and my companion chuckled.

"Elk. Not as many left these days. They weathered wolves and fire and everything else nature could throw at 'em, but men get greedy." He shrugged. "Can't blame 'em, I guess."

I was not sure if he wished to blame the men or the elk. "They are beautiful."

"They're critters." He fell silent again.

After a time, shifting uncomfortably on the hard board seat, I dared to ask, "How far is it to our destination?" Bringing up the name Conconully did not seem like a good idea, given his reaction to my first mention of it, but for all I knew we could be traveling for days. I was not prepared for sleeping out in the open, not to mention alone in the middle of nowhere except for someone I knew nothing about except his name and Jean's confidence. But she hadn't seen him for years. People did change.

He smiled down at me. He really was a rather large man, and I should have been frightened of him. I knew I should not be alone with him out here, on our way to a place he did not seem to want to admit even existed, but here I was. A sudden and inexplicable feeling of safety and warmth enveloped me.

Mr. Miller chuckled. "My wife would have liked you."

Taken aback, I said, "Would have?" and immediately regretted the question.

His face closed down and he made quite the affair of reaching into his pocket for a handkerchief and blowing his nose while hanging onto the reins. I would have offered to take them while he managed the business, but while the eight mules were still pacing along in perfect harmony, I had no illusions about being able to control them if that situation should change.

He did not answer me. He had not answered either of my questions, in point of fact.

"I am sorry for your loss," I said to the air in general, and listened to the grass sweeping the sides of the wagon as the only reply I received.

When the sun had reached far above the hills and beamed bright but unwarming light down upon us, Mr. Miller brought the mules to a stop near the creek we had been following for about an hour. "Need to rest and feed."

I assumed he meant the animals, but he also brought out a parcel tucked into the back of the wagon and handed it to me before he went to unhitch the team.

Surprised, I opened the parcel, and could feel my eyes widen. Inside the bundle was more than enough food for two, and such food! Fried chicken still crispy even though cold, creamy potato salad, and a jar of preserved peaches. And underneath these riches, protected by a stoneware plate, sat two large pieces of apple pie.

"Oh, my," was all I could think to say. My mouth was watering. The breakfast I had choked down at the hotel this morning seemed days ago. I had forgotten what appetite was like. It felt wonderful.

Mr. Miller looked up from where he was tending his mules and grinned. "Audrey's a good cook."

Was Audrey his wife? But no, that made no sense. I knew better than to ask. Once he climbed back up on the wagon seat, I spread the cloth our picnic had come wrapped in on the bench between us, and we both tucked in.

Impossibly, the food tasted even better than it looked. Between the two of us, we polished off every bit. I looked at my companion and said, without thinking, "If you eat like this every day, it surprises me you're not too heavy for the mules."

He burst out laughing, and I added, embarrassed, "It must be all the hard work." He nodded, still smiling, and I smiled back at him, feeling brave once more. "How much farther to our destination?"

He frowned, but not, it seemed, at me. "It's hard to tell."

How could he not know? I tried to think of a way to phrase it that would not cause him to close down again. "You must know how many miles it is from Omak to," I paused, still unwilling to risk saying the name, "our destination. And have at least a rough idea of how far we've traveled. Surely this isn't the first time you have made this trip."

He shook his head. At last he said, "I'm not so good with that kind of thing anymore."

An unease crept over me. "Surely you're not lost! You've been following the tracks..." I turned to stare back at the road we'd been following. Granted, it had become only two wheel tracks through the tall grass not long after we had left Omak, but those tracks had been distinct. Now, as I stared back the way we had come, I could see nothing. No wheel marks, no mule dung, not a single sign anyone had ever come this way, let alone a heavily-loaded wagon, eight mules, and two people.

Before I could turn back to him and ask all the questions boiling in my mind, Mr. Miller said, "Be right back. Got to–" he gestured.

He climbed down and disappeared behind some trees. I waited. What else could I do? He was simply answering a call of nature. I had done so myself earlier, catching up to the wagon as it rolled along slowly when I was finished.

But it was a long time before he finally came back, and when he did, his entire demeanor told me I would get no answers, quiz him as I might.

My uneasiness increased. I wished I had not given in to Jean's insistence. I wished I had never left Seattle. I wished I'd had somewhere else to go. But, as my mother used to say, if wishes were horses, then beggars could ride. I was here because it was the only option open to me. And, I had to admit, because Jean had been so convinced it would be the saving of me. It only went to show that she refused to believe the specialist, or thought I had not been honest when I told her what the specialist had said.

"Did you know my friend Jean?" I asked him. He now felt like a brick wall sitting beside me. "She grew up in Conconully." Silence. "I know you recognized her family name." Silence.

I took a deep breath. "Please, Mr. Miller. Perhaps you were right and I made a terrible mistake, asking you to take me to Conconully. Please talk to me. Tell me where we are and how much farther we have to go."

He suddenly straightened and relaxed. "Not much farther."

I sighed relief. Then we came around a bend in the creek and over a rise.

"Well," Mr. Miller said. "Here we are."

CHAPTER 4

"Here?" I croaked, and cleared my throat. "Where?"

Mr. Miller shrugged. "Conconully. What did you expect?"

"But–" I could say no more.

"You can't say I didn't warn you." He climbed down and went to the mules, taking the harness of the right lead animal and guiding it around in a circle so the wagon was facing the other way. Then he came to me, holding up his hands as if to help me down.

I did not move, to take them or to do anything else.

He shifted his feet. "This is as far as I go." The sadness was back in his eyes. No, not sadness, grief. Why, or who was he grieving?

"Where is the town?" I asked in bewilderment.

"Flood. Didn't you read about it? It was in all the papers when it happened." He lowered his arms and shrugged.

It didn't look like a flood had passed through here. It didn't look like anything had ever happened here. Only an open meadow, ringed with forest. "Why didn't you tell me?"

"Figgered you knew. Figgered your friend told you." He went around to the back of the wagon. I assumed he would come around to the other side and climb back on, take us on to wherever he was carting his load. Instead he began unloading, tilting and rolling the barrels as if they were much lighter than they had been when he'd first filled the wagon with them back in Omak. Or as if he was much stronger. The thought came to me unbidden and I shook it away as nonsensical. If anything, after a long day's ride, he should have been more tired. But his back was straighter and his arms were corded with muscle.

"What are you doing?" I asked, even though it was obvious.

He did not answer me. I climbed down and went to the back of the wagon. "Why are you unloading here?"

Wordlessly he pulled my valise from under the board bench and handed it to me, then spoke. "You wanted me to bring you to Conconully. You're here. My job's done." He looked as if he wanted to say something else, but thought better of it. Then he opened his mouth again as if he couldn't help himself. "Tell Rose– tell Rose I miss her."

I stared at him. "But no one is here!"

He did not answer me, but before long the wagon was empty and the barrels were neatly stacked on the rough meadow. He climbed back up onto the wagon seat. I tried to lift my valise, to put it back in the wagon, but a stab of pain hit me and I dropped it.

"You cannot leave me here!" Ignoring the sudden agony, I tried to scramble back aboard without my valise, but Mr. Miller shook the reins, and the mules began to move. I fell back before my foot was caught in the slowly spinning wheel spokes.

"Wait! Please!" I ran to follow it. "Don't leave me!"

The wagon, moving much faster now that it was empty, crested the rise and disappeared behind it before I could catch up. But when I reached the top myself, the wagon, the mules, and Mr. Miller were gone.

Not simply headed back where he had come from, but vanished, as if they had never been there in the first place. I sank to my knees in the tall grass and put my head in my hands. It was what I deserved for having gone off on this wild goose chase in the first place, I supposed. For listening to Jean in the first place.

But I'd had no one else to listen to, and nowhere else to go. She'd made it clear I shouldn't – couldn't – come back. I could understand that. Unemployed, ill, with no prospects, I would have been nothing but a weight on her and her resources. She'd owed me nothing, and yet she had, I thought, given me far more than I could have expected from her. She'd even said coming here would give me a prospect. But to do this to me?

Perhaps she hadn't known. Even as the thought passed through my mind, however, I dismissed it. She was a journalist. She not only followed the news, she reported on it, took it and made it her own. Yes, Conconully was – had been – a small town in the back of beyond, but it had been her hometown. She'd have read about the flood. She'd have known.

She'd sent me on a wild goose chase to nowhere. I wondered what she was thinking of me now, if she wondered if I'd caught onto her cruel joke. Send a dying woman to a dead town? Why? And spend her precious funds on my journey?

Now the only person who knew where I'd been abandoned was the man who'd left me here. The man who had utterly vanished, whose wagon and mules did not leave a trace of where they had passed.

I had no idea how to find my way back to Omak, let alone Seattle. And I had no one to blame but myself.

I lifted my head from my hands and stared at my surroundings, unseeing at first, then, though I'd have thought it wasn't possible to be more wounded and flummoxed than I already was, with an ever-growing sense of disbelief.

Nothing was right. Nothing made sense. Even the tiniest details were off.

It was late November. By rights my clothing should be wet with snow, and I starting to worry about frostbite. Instead I was almost too warm in my heavy woolens, hood, coat, scarf, and boots. I threw the hood back and let the sunshine beam its warmth down on my head – yes, the sky had been cloudless all day, but the sun had been so low as to feel like the perpetual sunset which was all winter ever gave us this far north. Now it was almost directly overhead, and I was perspiring.

I pulled off my gloves and unbuttoned my coat. After another moment, I took it off altogether and spread it over the grass to sit down and try to think what to do next.

The soft, supple, green grass of spring, not the dry brown broom bristles of winter. I glanced up to see enormous maple trees scattered across the meadow, their soft red-tinged green leaves beginning to accordion themselves open. Along the edge of the forest, shining new pale green needles on the larch trees glowed against the darker pines and firs.

It was as I was staring in wonder at this vision of spring in November that I first heard the voices. Not just one, but several, ranging from a deep male baritone to an unexpectedly authoritative-sounding soprano, all having what seemed from their tones to be a lighthearted conversation, although I could not make out the words.

I cannot explain how absolute the relief I felt was. I was not stranded here alone after all. I didn't know where the voices came from, or why these people were here. All that mattered was that I was not utterly abandoned, that I would survive, that they would help me. Help me do what or go where, I had no idea, but at the moment that was completely beside the point.

"Hello?" I called eagerly.

The voices stopped. Not only the voices, but everything. Utter silence reigned around me. The bitter wind yanked at my scarf, and, no, I cannot explain it, but suddenly I was back in the middle of winter once more.

I could have wept, but it would do me no good. Braced against the ache in my abdomen, I stood and pulled my coat back on. The least I could do was go fetch my valise. Then I would find those people and ask, no, demand for them to help me.

As I made my way down the slope, the wind died down again, and suddenly I was back in spring. I could not hear the voices, although I vow I sensed, felt, knew I was not alone. I found my valise where I had left it. I picked it up with no trouble. Its weight was normal, even light, in my hand, not agonizingly heavy as it had been when I'd tried to put it in Mr. Miller's wagon.

The barrels were not as they had been when I left them behind. Not that I had paid them much attention at the time, but it had only been less than an hour, if that.

There'd been over two dozen barrels, all on end, all neatly stacked as if in a warehouse waiting for someone to come get them. Now, three of them lay on their sides, some little distance from the others, again in a tidy row.

I shook my head. Something was wrong, but it was not with my surroundings. This had to be some sort of dream. I must be still back in the little house in Seattle, in my bed, with Jean in hers in the next room breathing heavily in her sleep.

I was hearing breathing, but I was not dreaming. I was not in my bed in our– Jean's house in Seattle. I was out in the woods alone, far from anywhere with no hope of finding my way back.

"Please?" I called out desperately. "I know you're out there. I need your help."

A throat cleared behind me. I started violently and whirled around, dropping my valise with a thump.

A short, stout man in elegant clothing of the style of twenty years ago stood in front of me. He smiled at me in what I could not help but see as genial approval. "Hello, young lady. My name is Max Pepper. How may I be of assistance?"

I opened my mouth, but I could not find my voice. I swallowed and closed it again. It was as though he had appeared out of nowhere.

His expression changed to one of concern. "Are you ill? Let me fetch the doctor–"

I swallowed again. "No." No, I was not fine, but Jean had told me to find Max Pepper, and, glory be, I'd found him. I took a deep breath and let it out in relief "Where am I?"

He answered me with a question of his own. "How did you come to arrive here?"

Honesty was the best policy, especially with a potential employer. "Jean Clancy sent me. I came on the wagon that brought those barrels."

This gained me a completely unexpected reaction. His eyes went wide and he took a step back. And another. And another.

Before I could say anything to stop him, he was gone.

He was not gone long, however. Before I could think of what to do, whether to try to follow him or wait or panic, he had returned. And when he came back he was not alone. With him were a tall, angular, middle-aged woman; an older man judging by the color of his steel-gray hair; a tall young man with brown hair and a sheriff's star pinned to the chest pocket of his plaid shirt; and a short young blonde woman carrying a black leather bag and wearing men's trousers.

They all wore the same astonished expression, but, as I watched them, it changed to varying degrees of pleasure. Mr. Pepper looked positively smug as he observed his companions.

Before he could say anything, however, the sheriff stepped forward and held out his hand. Not knowing what else to do, I took it. His fingers were warm, even through my glove. He frowned, and turned to the blonde girl? woman? in her odd clothing. "Amy, she's freezing. We need to get her to town."

A strange lassitude had overtaken me at the touch of his hand. "I-I need to sit down," I told him, their figures wavering in front of me, and, I am ashamed to admit, I fainted dead onto the grass.

I do not believe I was "out," as the sheriff called it later, for long. When I awoke, I was riding between the older man and the sheriff, down the hill, in a sort of chair carry with their hands laced together underneath me and behind my back.

I struggled to get down, but the sheriff said, "It's all right. We won't drop you."

"I don't think that's what's worrying her, Dan," said the tall woman. She was right, of course, but only partly. I'd never felt so weak in my life, as if I hadn't slept or eaten for days.

"Please let me down," I asked, in spite of this.

I wished we'd been introduced properly, so I could demand it of them by name. The sheriff looked over at the blonde woman as if asking for permission.

"It would probably be better for her if you did," said the young woman. So they gently set me down on my feet. The older man held onto my arm. I suppose I looked as if I would fall over again at any instant, although I did feel a bit better now.

"Let go, Rob," the young woman said decisively. "She'll be stronger if you let her alone."

Scowling, the tall man did so. I swayed slightly, and he made as if to take hold of me again, but did not. And, oddly enough, I felt better standing on my own two feet, without support, which pleased me very much.

Mr. Pepper seemed pleased, too, and answered my unspoken wish, gesturing to each person in turn. "This is our sheriff, Dan Reilly, and our doctor, Amy Duvall, and Audrey and Rob Missel. And you are, Miss?"

Oh. The young woman was a doctor? I supposed that explained the black bag and the pulse-taking and all, but not the trousers. She certainly didn't look like any doctors of my acquaintance. Decidedly not like Dr. Spencer or the specialist. The more I considered that, however, the more it stood in Dr. Duvall's favor. "My name is Claudia Ogden."

"Well, then, Miss Ogden, if you're feeling up to it, why don't you come back to town with us?"

The relief was almost overwhelming. Town. There was a town. I had found Max Pepper and there was a town. "All right." I took one step, then another, and another, and before I knew it I was striding along with them on a dirt road that had appeared beneath our feet as if out of nowhere, alongside the chiming stream.

But something was missing– I stopped dead. "My valise! I need to go back and get my valise!"

"It's all right," Mr. Pepper told me. "The men have to go back and fetch the barrels. They'll bring your valise with them."

"My handbag!"

Mrs. Missel held out her hand. "I presume this belongs to you, then." I all but snatched the bag from her, then blushed, embarrassed at my rudeness.

She smiled at me. "It's all right. You've been through the bit of a shock, and there's more to come. We're very glad to meet you."

"Thank you." I paused, making the connection. "Are you the fine cook whose delicious fried chicken I ate on my way here?"

She positively beamed at me. "Why, yes, I am."

I did not begin to know what I should ask next. But no one had answered the most important question I had, and it came out more plaintively than I had intended. "Then perhaps you can tell me, please, where on earth we are?"

They were all smiling at me now. I wished I knew why. But as we rounded a bend and came over a slight rise in the road, the valley opened out, and in front of us sat what must have once been a prosperous town.

Prosperous no more, however. Nothing remained but tumbledown ruins scattered across the valley in a peculiarly orderly fashion, along what must have been a grid of streets but was now nothing but ruts in the green grass. Silvery wood lay strewn hither and yon, glass shards of broken windows glinting in the bright spring sunshine.

I stared at it, then at my companions. Two of them, Sheriff Reilly and Dr. Duvall, gazed back at me in what I can only call commiseration. The other three seemed not to notice my astonishment, although Mr. Pepper's smugness had not disappeared.

What has he to be smug about? I wondered wildly. Jean, what have you gotten me into?

As I gaped down at what I could only call a ghost town, Mr. Pepper swept his arm grandly at it, a strangely proprietary gesture. "Welcome to Conconully," he said proudly.

Reunion is available at all major retailers.

Books by M.M. Justus

Tales of the Unearthly Northwest

Sojourn

"New Year's Eve in Conconully"

Reunion

Time in Yellowstone

Repeating History

True Gold

"Homesick"

Finding Home

Much Ado in Montana

Cross-Country: Adventures Alone Across America and Back

About the Author

M.M. Justus spent most of her childhood summers in the back seat of a car, traveling with her parents to almost every national park west of the Mississippi and a great many places in between.

She holds degrees in British and American literature and history and library science, and a certificate in museum studies. In her other life, she's held jobs as far flung as hog farm bookkeeper, music school secretary, professional dilettante (aka reference librarian), and museum curator, all of which are fair fodder for her fiction.

Her other interests include quilting, gardening, meteorology, and the travel bug she inherited from her father. She lives on the rainy side of the Cascade mountains in Washington state, within easy reach of all of its mysterious places.

Please visit her website and blog at http://mmjustus.com, on Facebook at https://www.facebook.com/M.M.Justusauthor, on Twitter @mmjustus, or on Pinterest at http://www.pinterest.com/justus1240/.

Made in the USA
Columbia, SC
15 November 2017